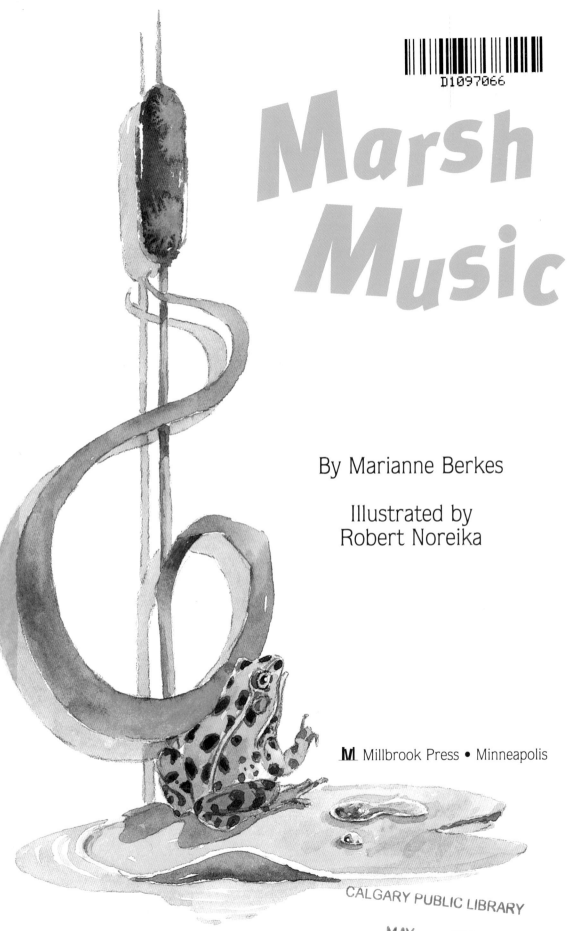

Marsh Music

By Marianne Berkes

Illustrated by
Robert Noreika

M Millbrook Press • Minneapolis

To my daughter, Melissa.
And in joyful memory of my parents,
Anne & Harry Staffhorst,
who filled my life with many songs.
—MB

To Sarah, Chris, and my father.
—RN

Millbrook Press, Inc.
A division of Lerner Publishing Group, Inc.
241 First Avenue North
Minneapolis, MN 55401 U.S.A.

Website address: www.lernerbooks.com

Library of Congress Cataloging-in-Publication Data
Berkes, Marianne.
Marsh music/by Marianne Berkes;
illustrated by Robert Noreika.
p. cm.
Summary: During the night, the marsh comes alive
with the singing of all kinds of frogs, from spring peepers
and wood frogs to leopard and pig frogs.
ISBN 978-0-7613-1850-7 (lib. bdg.)
[1. Frogs—Fiction. 2. Animal sounds—Fiction. 3. Stories in rhyme.]
I.Noreika, Robert, ill. II. Title.
PZ8.3. B4557 2000
[E]—dc21   99-051641

Manufactured in the United States of America
6 – DP – 12/15/10

"Frogs do for the night
what birds do for the day;
they give it a voice.
And the voice is
a varied and stirring one
that ought to be better known."

—Dr. Archie Carr,
The Everglades

The rain has stopped.
Night is coming.
The pond awakes with
quiet humming.

Maestro frog hops to the mound
As night begins to fill with sound.

Peepers peep *pe-ep*, *peep*, *peep*.
They have had a good day's sleep!

Spring
peepers

Chorus frogs are hard to see.
Hear them chirping *do re mi.*

Then the other frogs come in.
Soon the concert will begin.

Chorus
frogs

Fireflies light up the stage
as the maestro turns the pag

Maestro raises his baton.
Now it's time to carry on.

The woodwinds whistle a l o n g, sweet trill.

The strings go
twang,
twang,
twang.

The horns bleat loudly
whaaa,
whaaa,
whaaa,

Percussions snap
and bang.

Green frogs

Wood
frogs

American
toads

Narrow-
mouthed
toads

Maestro starts out kind of slow.
They're playing in "adagio."

Then he motions to the bass.
The tempo starts to change.
They're playing at a faster pace
And in a higher range.

Pig
frogs

Green
tree
frogs

Longer notes. Shorter notes.
Listen to the quarter notes.

Woink-woink-woink
Woink-woink-woink
Three-quarter time.

Gronk-gronk-gronk
Gronk-gronk-gronk
Music sublime.

Two leopard frogs
leap through the air.
They're dancing a ballet

Leopard
frogs

They pirouette on lily pads
And then they swim away.

Barking
tree
frog

A tree frog glides onto a frond
As sounds keep rising from the pond.

"Aarf, aarf," he calls down from the tree
And joins the outdoor symphony.

Stars are twinkling to the tune
As they dance around the moon.

The orchestra plays "moderato."
Maestro motions "animato."

Faster, louder, wondrous sounds.
Music of the night abounds!

There is a pause—then wild applause.
Bravo! Encore! We want some more!"

But now it's dawn.
The stars are gone.
Maestro puts down his baton.

That's all my friends.
It's time to go.
Tonight there'll be
another show.

The marsh is quiet.
No more ringing.
But wait, I think
I hear some singing!

The day's awake. Now it's morning.
A melody is heard!
Can't be frogs, 'cause they're asleep.
I think I hear . . .

. . . a bird!

Glossary
of Musical Terms

Adagio	slowly
Animato	to play with vigor
Baton	a slender stick the leader uses to direct the orchestra.
Horns	the brass section of the orchestra. Brass instruments are: trumpets, French horns, trombones, and tubas.
Maestro	conductor or teacher of music
Moderato	to play with moderation of tempo
Percussion	Percussion instruments are: drums, cymbals, bells, triangles, harp, and piano.
Pirouette	a whirling around on one foot or the point of a toe, especially in ballet
Quarter note	a musical note with the time value of one quarter of a whole note
Strings	the largest section of the orchestra. String instruments are: violins, violas, cellos, double basses.
Symphony	consonance of sounds: a concert
Tempo	the speed at which a musical composition is performed
Three-quarter time	usually a waltz where the accent is on the first beat
Woodwinds	Woodwind instruments are: flutes, clarinets, oboes and bassoon.

The Cast

"Maestro" Bullfrog (3½ to 8 inches/9 to 20 cm) North America's largest frog species, bullfrogs are yellowish green to black, sometimes mottled with dark spots. Bullfrogs call a deep, resonant "jug-o-rum" that can be heard for long distances. They are strictly aquatic and can be found in lakes and ponds.

Spring Peepers (¾ to 1⅜ inches/1.9 to 3.5 cm) are small, slender brown or olive-gray frogs with pointed heads. They breed in swamps and live in low bushes and plants. When they sing in full chorus, their sharp, high-pitched series of whistles and trills, pe-ep, pe-ep, pe-ep, can be deafening!

Chorus Frogs (¾ to 1⅜ inches/1.9 to 3.5 cm) are gray with dark spots and often blend in with their surroundings. They have slim bodies and pointed snouts, and sound like a comb clicking. The upland chorus frog has a "vibrating" chirp, while the ornate chorus frog has a clear long chirp.

American Toads (2 to 4⅜ inches/5 to 11 cm) Short and fat in body, toads come in a variety of color, usually brown, gray, olive, or red with various-sized warts. The American toad's song sounds like a sweet trilling whistle. It is a sustained trill that sounds like "bu-rr-r-r."

Green Frogs (2 to 4 inches/5 to 10 cm) live in swamps and ponds in the eastern United States. They are usually greenish brown with a bright green mask from the tympanum (eardrum) toward the jaw. Their call sounds like the plucking of a string bass or the twang of a rubber band slightly stretched over an open box.

Narrow-mouthed Toads ($^7/_8$ to $1^1/_2$ inches/2.2 to 3.8 cm) are dark-colored with small heads and pointed snouts. This tiny toad's loud "whaaa" sounds like a bleating sheep. Nocturnal, a lover of rain and moist areas, the narrow-mouthed toad calls from shallow water with rear feet submerged and forefeet planted on the bank.

Wood Frogs ($1^1/_2$ to $3^1/_4$ inches/3.5 to 8.3 cm) are often a bright metallic copper color with dark masks over their eyes. They live in woodlands, except when they go to and from marshes to breed. Vocalizing males make short, raspy, ducklike sounds: a sharp, snappy, clack— 2, 4, or 6 notes in succession.

Pig Frogs ($3^1/_4$ to 6 inches/8 to 15 cm) are similar to bullfrogs and are brownish olive to gray with a creamy-colored underside netted with a brownish pattern. The tops of their heads are dark green. Strictly aquatic, pig frogs call from lily pads and sound like pigs grunting: woink, woink, woink.

Green Tree Frogs ($1^1/_2$ to $2^1/_2$ inches/3.5 to 6 cm) are especially active on damp or rainy evenings and are easily seen around the edges of ponds and lakes, particularly among cattails. Slender and smooth, the beautiful bright-green tree frog has a light stripe along its upper jaw and side. Its call is: gronk, gronk, gronk.

Leopard Frogs (2 to 4 inches/5 to 10 cm) are slender and smooth skinned. They vary in color from light brown to dark green with leopardlike brown spots. Found around any body of water, their unusually long hind legs allow them to launch into the air, soaring great distances. The leopard frog's call is long and low, interspersed with clucking grunts.

Barking Tree Frogs (2 to $2^3/_4$ inches/5 to 7 cm) This is our largest native tree frog, green to greenish brown, its back covered with round brown spots. Quite pudgy in build and one of the most colorful tree frogs, a breeding chorus of barking tree frogs sounds like dogs barking.

About the Author and Illustrator

Marianne Berkes was an early childhood educator and also directed children's theater in Pawling, New York, before moving to Florida where she is a children's librarian. "Miss Marianne," as she is known to the children in the Palm Beach County Library System, enjoys telling stories about frogs and nature. She lives in Hobe Sound with her husband, Roger. The cacophony of sounds she often hears from the pond in back of their home served as the inspiration for this, her first book.

An award-winning member of the Connecticut Watercolor Society and the Salmagundi Club in New York City, Robert Noreika also teaches classes throughout the New England region. He enjoys long treks in the woods with his family. Noreika and his wife have one daughter; they live in Rocky Hill, Connecticut.